For my mother with love. / Para mi madre, con amor —L.M.

*For Sam in Sydney, happy 4th birthday, with all my love /
Para Sam en Sydney, feliz cuarto cumpleaños, con todo mi amor.*
—M.R.

BABY RATTLESNAKE

VIBORITA DE CASCABEL

Cuento de / Told by
TE ATA

Adaptación de / Adapted by
LYNN MORONEY

Ilustraciones de / Illustrated by
MIRA REISBERG

Children's Book Press, *an imprint of* Lee & Low Books Inc.
New York

Out in the place where the rattlesnakes lived,
there was a little baby rattlesnake who cried
all the time because he did not have a rattle.

Allá en el lugar donde las víboras de cascabel
vivían, había una viborita bebé que lloraba
todo el tiempo porque no tenía cascabel.

He said to his mother and father, "I don't know why I don't have a rattle. I'm made just like my brother and sister. How can I be a rattlesnake if I don't have a rattle?"

Mother and Father Rattlesnake said, "You are too young to have a rattle. When you get to be as old as your brother and sister, you will have a rattle, too."

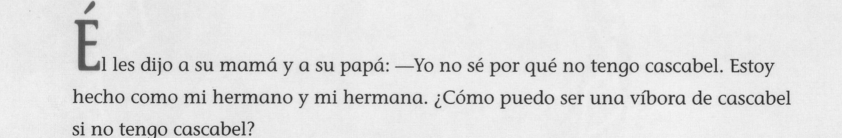

Él les dijo a su mamá y a su papá: —Yo no sé por qué no tengo cascabel. Estoy hecho como mi hermano y mi hermana. ¿Cómo puedo ser una víbora de cascabel si no tengo cascabel?

Mamá y Papá Víbora de Cascabel le dijeron: —Estás muy joven para tener cascabel. Cuando crezcas más y tengas la edad de tu hermano y tu hermana, entonces tú tendrás también un cascabel.

But Baby Rattlesnake did not want
to wait. So he just cried and cried. He shook
his tail and when he couldn't hear a rattle
sound, he cried even louder.

Mother and Father said,
"Shhh! Shhh! Shhhhh!"
Brother and Sister said,
"Shhh! Shhh! Shhhhh!"

Pero Viborita de Cascabel no quería esperar. Así fue que se puso a llorar y a llorar. Sacudía la cola y cuando no oía sonar un cascabel, lloraba aún más fuerte. Su mamá y su papá le dijeron:

—¡Shhh! ¡Shhh! ¡Shhhhh!

Su hermano y su hermana le dijeron:

—¡Shhh! ¡Shhh! ¡Shhhhh!

But Baby Rattlesnake wouldn't stop crying. He kept the Rattlesnake People awake all night.

Pero Viborita de Cascabel no dejaba de llorar. Así mantenía despierta a la Gente Víbora durante toda la noche.

The next morning, the Rattlesnake People called a big council. They talked and they talked just like people do, but they couldn't decide how to make that little baby rattlesnake happy. He didn't want anything else but a rattle.

At last one of the elders said, "Go ahead, give him a rattle. He's just too young and he'll get into trouble. But let him learn a lesson. I just want to get some sleep."

So they gave Baby Rattlesnake a rattle.

A la siguiente mañana, la Gente Víbora se reunió en un gran concilio. Hablaron y hablaron como la gente lo hace, pero no se ponían de acuerdo en qué hacer para contentar a la viborita bebé porque lo único que quería la viborita era un cascabel.

Por fin uno de los ancianos habló: —Decídanse de una vez. Denle un cascabel. Él es muy joven y se meterá en líos. Pero dejemos que él aprenda una lección. Lo que quiero es otra vez poder dormir.

Así fue cómo le dieron el cascabel a Viborita de Cascabel.

Baby Rattlesnake loved his rattle. He shook his tail and for the first time he heard, "Ch-Ch-Ch! Ch-Ch-Ch!" He was so excited!

He sang a rattle song, "Ch-Ch-Ch! Ch-Ch-Ch!"

He danced a rattle dance, "Ch-Ch-Ch! Ch-Ch-Ch!"

Viborita de cascabel se enamoró de su cascabel. Sacudió la colita y por primera vez oyó: «¡Ch-Ch-Ch! ¡Ch-ch-ch!» ¡Estaba muy entusiasmado!

Luego tocó una canción con el cascabel: «¡Ch-Ch-Ch! ¡Ch-Ch-Ch!»

Luego bailó una danza con el cascabel: «¡Ch-Ch-Ch! ¡Ch-Ch-Ch!»

15

Soon Baby Rattlesnake learned to play tricks with his rattle. He hid in the rocks and when small animals came by, he darted out rattling, "Ch-Ch-Ch! Ch-Ch-Ch!"

He made old Jack Rabbit jump.

He made Old Man Turtle jump.

He made Prairie Dog jump.

Each time Baby Rattlesnake laughed and laughed.

He thought it was fun to scare the Animal People.

ch ch
ch ch ch

Pronto Viborita de Cascabel aprendió a hacer trucos con el cascabel. Se escondía entre las rocas y cuando pasaban los animalitos, los sorprendía haciendo sonar su cascabel: «¡Ch-Ch-Ch! ¡Ch-Ch-Ch!»

Así hizo saltar al Conejo del Campo.

Así hizo saltar al Anciano Tortuga.

Así hizo saltar al Perrito Llanero.

Y cada vez, Viborita de Cascabel se reía y se reía. Pensaba que era divertido asustar a la Gente Animal.

Mother and Father warned Baby Rattlesnake,
"You must not use your rattle in such a way."

Big Brother and Big Sister said,
"You are not being careful with your rattle."

The Rattlesnake People told Baby Rattlesnake to
stop acting so foolish with his rattle.

Baby Rattlesnake did not listen.

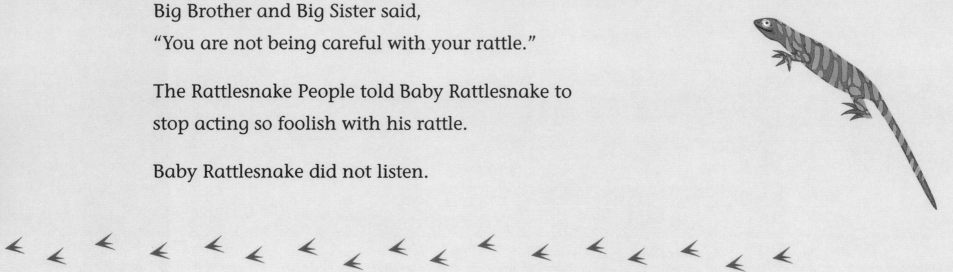

Su mamá y su papá le advirtieron a Viborita de Cascabel:
—No debes usar el cascabel de esa manera.

Su hermano y su hermana mayor le dijeron:
—Tú no eres cuidadoso con el cascabel.

La Gente Víbora de Cascabel le dijo a Viborita de Cascabel
que dejara de actuar de ese modo tan tonto con el cascabel.

Pero Viborita de Cascabel no les escuchaba.

One day, Baby Rattlesnake said to his mother and father,
"How will I know a chief's daughter when I see her?"
"Well, she's usually very beautiful and walks with her head held high," said Father.
"And she's very neat in her dress," added Mother.
"Why do you want to know?" asked Father.
"Because I want to scare her!" said Baby Rattlesnake. And he started off down the path before his mother and father could warn him never to do a thing like that.

Un día, Viborita de Cascabel les preguntó a su mamá y a su papá:
—¿Cómo puedo reconocer a la hija de un jefe si la veo?
—Bueno, por lo general, es muy hermosa y camina con la cara levantada
—dijo su papá.
—Y lleva un vestido muy limpio y hermoso —añadió su mamá.
—¿Por qué quieres saber? —preguntó su papá.
—¡Porque quiero asustarla! —dijo Viborita de Cascabel. Y se fue por el camino antes de que su mamá y su papá le pudieran advertir que nunca hiciera tal cosa.

The little fellow reached the place where the Indians traveled. He curled himself up on a log and he started rattling, "Ch-Ch-Ch!" He was having a wonderful time.

All of a sudden he saw a beautiful maiden coming toward him from a long way off. She walked with her head held high, and she was very neat in her dress.

"Ah," thought Baby Rattlesnake. "She must be the chief's daughter."

El pequeño llegó al lugar por donde pasaban los indios. Se enroscó en un tronco y comenzó a sonar su cascabel: «¡Ch-Ch-Ch!» Se divertía muchísimo.

De pronto vio a una hermosa joven que venía desde una gran distancia hacia donde estaba él. La joven caminaba con la cara levantada y llevaba un vestido muy limpio y hermoso.

«¡Ajá» pensó Viborita de Cascabel. «Ésta debe ser la hija del jefe.»

Baby Rattlesnake hid in the rocks. He was excited.
This was going to be his best trick.

He waited and waited. The chief's daughter came closer and closer.

When she was in just the right spot, he darted out of the rocks.

"Ch-Ch-Ch-Ch-Ch!"

Viborita de Cascabel se escondió entre las rocas.
Estaba entusiasmadísimo. Éste iba a ser su mejor truco.

Esperó y esperó. La hija del jefe se acercaba más y más.
Cuando ella llegó al lugar exacto, Viborita de Cascabel
salió de repente de las rocas.

«¡Ch-Ch-Ch-Ch-Ch!»

"HO!"

cried the chief's daughter. She whirled around, stepping
on Baby Rattlesnake's rattle and crushing it to pieces.

—¡JO!

—gritó la hija del jefe. La joven dio una vuelta de repente, y
le pisó el cascabel a Viborita de Cascabel, haciéndolo trizas.

Baby Rattlesnake looked at his beautiful rattle scattered all over the trail. He didn't know what to do.

He took off for home as fast as he could.

Viborita de Cascabel miró el hermoso cascabel hecho trizas por todo el camino. No sabía qué hacer.

Tan pronto como pudo se regresó a casa.

With great sobs, he told Mother and Father what had happened. They wiped his tears and gave him big rattlesnake hugs.

For the rest of that day, Baby Rattlesnake stayed safe and snug, close by his rattlesnake family.

Con grandes sollozos, les contó a su mamá y a su papá lo que había pasado. Ellos le secaron las lágrimas y le dieron grandes abrazos de víbora.

Durante el resto del día, Viborita de Cascabel se quedó muy seguro y muy cómodo al lado de su familia de víboras de cascabel.

About Baby Rattlesnake

Te Ata, whose name means "Bearer of the Morning," was an internationally acclaimed Chickasaw Indian storyteller. Born in the Oklahoma Territory in 1897, she was proclaimed Oklahoma State's first Oklahoma State treasure. She regaled audiences in the USA and Europe for more than 65 years, performing at the White House during the Roosevelt years.

Oklahoma storyteller **Lynn Moroney**, herself part Indian, had admired Te Ata for years and finally asked her permission to retell the story of Baby Rattlesnake. At first, Te Ata said no. But after hearing Lynn tell her own stories at a storytelling festival, Te Ata was so impressed that she gave Lynn her blessing to tell this story and pass it on to others as a book.

"Baby Rattlesnake is a teaching tale about what happens when you get something before you are ready for it. Subsequent to the original publication of this book, I learned that rather than being a Chickasaw story, its origin is in the oral literature of the Pawnee Nation. The traditional version of the story can be found in "Pawnee Music" by Frances Denmore, in the Smithsonian Bureau of American Ethnology, Bulletin 93 (1929) 107-8. I am most pleased to be able to share the correct origin of this well-loved tale."—Lynn Moroney, Oklahoma City

Artist **Mira Reisberg** fell in love with the story of Baby Rattlesnake the moment she heard it. Mira was born in Australia and has lived in the Southwest United States, the setting of *Baby Rattlesnake*. Her medium for this book is cut paper and gouache paints.

Special thanks to Bay Area storyteller Gay Ducey, who brought Lynn's original manuscript to Children's Book Press and then nurtured the original edition of *Baby Rattlesnake* through its completion. And our special thanks to Harriet Rohmer, David Schecter, Katherine Tillotson, and Laura Chastain.

Text copyright © 1989, 2003 by Lynn Moroney
Illustrations copyright © 1989, 2003 by Mira Reisberg
All rights reserved. No part of this book may be reproduced, transmitted, or stored in an information retrieval system in any form or by any means, electronic, mecahnical, photocopying, recording, or otherwsie, without written permission from the publisher. Children's Book Press, an imprint of LEE & LOW BOOKS Inc., 95 Madison Avenue, New York, NY 10016, leeandlow.com

Edited by Harriet Rohmer and Dana Goldberg
Spanish translation by Francisco X. Alarcón
Book design by Andrew Ogus and Dana Goldberg
Book prouction by The Kids at Our House

Manufactured in China by First Choice Printing Co., Ltd., March 2016
10 9 8 7 6 5
Second Edition

Library of Congress Cataloging-in-Publication Data
Ata, Te.
    Baby rattlesnake / told by Te Ata; adaptation by Lynne Moroney; illustrations by Mira Reisberg = Viborita de cascabel / cuento de Te Ata; adaptación de Lynn Moroney; ilustraciones de Mira Reisberg.
        p. cm.
    Summary: Willful Baby Rattlesnake throws tantrums in order to get his rattle before he's ready, but he misuses it and learns a lesson.
        ISBN 978-0-89239-188-2 (bilingual paperback)
1. Pawnee Indians—Folklore. 2. Rattlesnakes—Folklore. 3. Bilingual books. [1. Pawnee Indians—Folklore. 2. Rattlesnakes—Folklore. 3. Indians of North America—Southwest, New—Folklore. 4. Folklore— Southwest, New. 5. Spanish language materials—Bilingual.] I. Ata, Te. II. Reisberg, Mira, ill. III. Title.
E99.C55M67 2003
398.24'5279638'08997073—dc21
    [E]   2002041526